Mark Pett

LIZARD *from the* PARK

SIMON & SCHUSTER BOOKS FOR YOUNG READERS
New York   London   Toronto   Sydney   New Delhi

For Millie and Cleo,
who love both lizards and parks

SIMON & SCHUSTER BOOKS FOR YOUNG READERS
An imprint of Simon & Schuster Children's Publishing Division
1230 Avenue of the Americas, New York, New York 10020
Copyright © 2015 by Mark Pett
SIMON & SCHUSTER BOOKS FOR YOUNG READERS is a trademark of Simon & Schuster, Inc.
For information about special discounts for bulk purchases, please contact Simon & Schuster
Special Sales at 1-866-506-1949 or business@simonandschuster.com.
The Simon & Schuster Speakers Bureau can bring authors to your live event.
For more information or to book an event,
contact the Simon & Schuster Speakers Bureau at 1-866-248-3049
or visit our website at www.simonspeakers.com.
Book design by Lucy Ruth Cummins
The text for this book is set in 2011 Slimtype.
The illustrations for this book are rendered in charcoal and painted digitally.
Manufactured in China
1115 SCP
2 4 6 8 10 9 7 5 3
Library of Congress Cataloging-in-Publication Data
Pett, Mark, author, illustrator.
Lizard from the park / Mark Pett.
pages cm
Summary: When a lizard hatches from the egg Leonard finds in the park, he names it Buster
and takes it all around the city, but Buster grows bigger and bigger until Leonard realizes he
must devise a way to return his pet to the deepest, darkest part of the park and set him free.
ISBN 978-1-4424-8321-7 (hardcover)
ISBN 978-1-4424-8322-4 (eBook)
[1. Dinosaurs as pets—Fiction.] I. Title.
PZ7.P4478Liz 2015
[E]—dc23
2014040078

$\mathcal{L}$ike most days, Leonard walked home by himself. On this particular spring afternoon, he took a shortcut through the park.

When he got to the deepest, darkest part
of the park, Leonard spotted something.

It was an egg! And it was unlike any
egg Leonard had seen before.

Leonard put the egg in his backpack,
zipped it up, and carried it home.

He took it to his apartment, which was on the top floor of a very tall building.

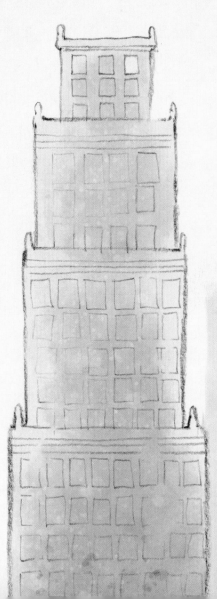

In his room, Leonard and the egg played together for the entire afternoon.

That night Leonard held the egg close as he fell asleep.

In the morning, Leonard noticed something.

The egg began to jiggle

and crack.

Then a nose
busted through
the shell.

It was a lizard! Leonard watched as the lizard busted through the rest of the shell. Then Leonard made a decision.

He named the lizard Buster.

Leonard couldn't wait to show his new friend the world outside.

He and Buster spent the whole day exploring
Leonard's favorite places in the city.

In the weeks following, Leonard took Buster everywhere.
They spent their mornings together, their afternoons together,

and they spent their in-betweens together.

As spring turned to summer, Leonard realized something: Not only did Buster keep growing

and growing

and growing,

but he seemed to
be enjoying himself
less and less.

Meanwhile, the bigger Buster got, the more Leonard had to disguise him so he would fit in among the city crowds.

It soon became impossible!

So Leonard decided to keep Buster in his room.

Buster didn't
seem to like
that, either.

Leonard moved him to the roof, though he knew it was only a matter of time before Buster would outgrow that, too.

After a while, Buster grew too big even for Leonard's room.

Leonard found himself in a
very difficult situation.

Finally, he had an idea.

He gathered every
balloon he could
find in the city:

red ones,

shiny ones,

balloons
shaped like
animals.

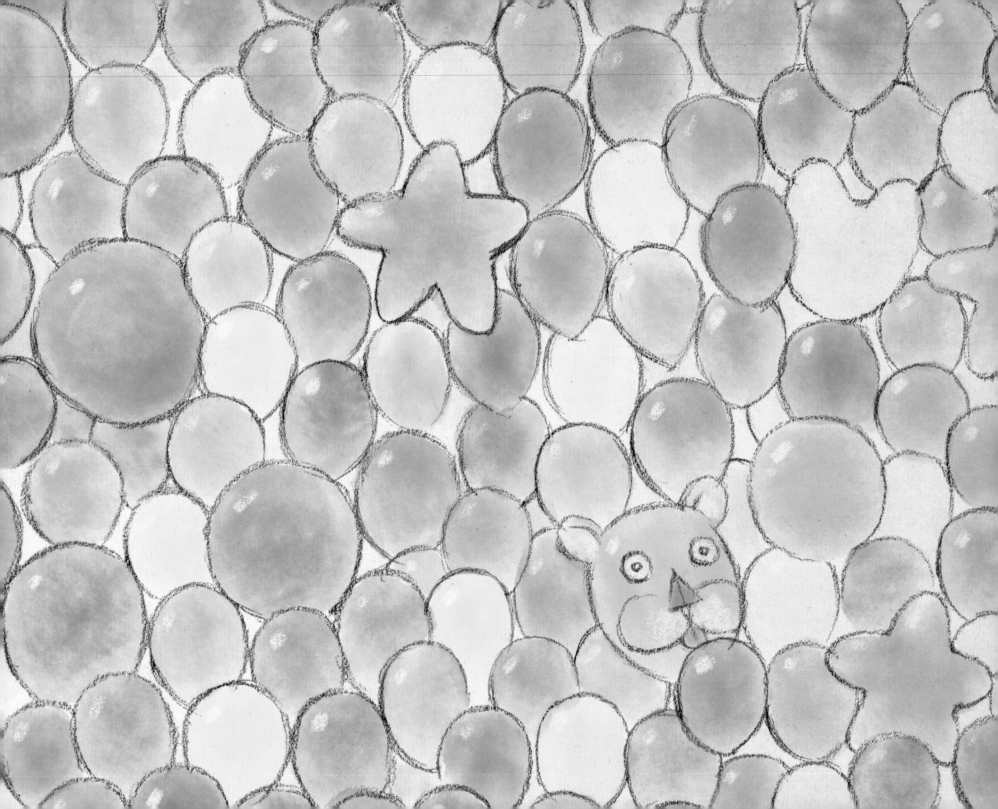

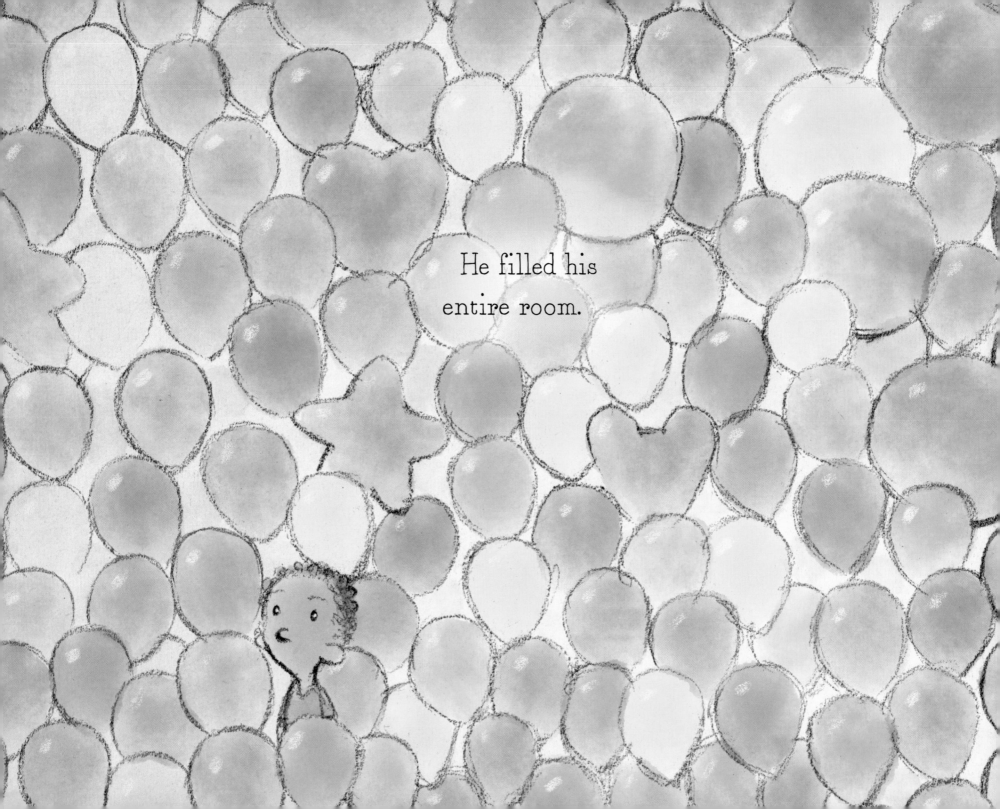

He filled his
entire room.

On the day of the big parade, noisy crowds gathered in the streets below.

Leonard heard music.

Then he saw the giant balloons.

Soon the parade reached his building.

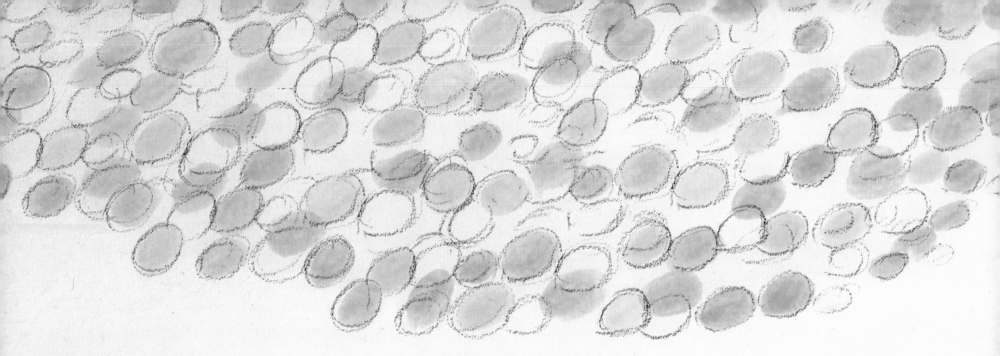

Leonard and Buster joined in.

When they reached the park,
Leonard and Buster floated
away from the parade

and set down gently near the deepest, darkest part of the park, where Buster joined his family.

Sometimes Leonard still cuts through
the park on his way home.

And sometimes he takes a new way.